To Meaghan,

This part of my Story / Li.

You to THANK. WITHOUT YOUR LOVE aND support

THERE WOULDN'T OF BeeN CloSURE To THE Dark

LURK.

"THANK You FOR Being THERE WHEN
I NEEDED you Most." - IV

ON Page <u>16</u> You WiLL FIND ONE

OF MaNY TeSTaMeNTS to THE iMpact

ON MY LiFe, MY writing aND MY HEart.

THat you HavE MADE.

-R IV

Winters Remnant

Winters Remnant

R.G. IV

To order additional copies of this book, contact:
Xlibris Corporation
1-888-795-4274
www.Xlibris.com
Orders@Xlibris.com
95800

<u>HELLO</u>

well first off, let me thank you for your interest in this tale. this first part is being released in the original format, my raw "UNCUT" version sort of speak. while reading this your're going to have many questions, i promise you when the time comes and this is all finished you'll get more insight into the inner workings of what i tried to express through these pages. with that said i will try to keep this brief as possible so you may read onward.

i know there are others like my-self, others who have felt and been to the darkest bounds of their hearts and feelings . . . those struggling the eternal war within . . . this is for you.

throughout the pages there are a lot of hidden secrets and anagrams that if solved will give you more insight to the memories.

there are also painful memories within the relapse from many experiences, it was immensely difficult to return to some of those times. many pieces of me are scattered throughout this as well, concealed to hopefully never to escape.

what you are about to read is not as much meant to be read with your mind, but felt with your heart.

that is it . . . so begin reading at any point and perhaps i will catch up with you on the other-side.

RGIV

~~THE START~~

I. this is the first of many sleepless nights, dreamless nights always haunted by shadows of my past;my lost. i can't sleep anymore, they continue to haunt and torture. my tears of regret flood my head,and plague rememberd memories. i can only say that i see things, evil things.

WHY DO THEY COME ONLY TO ME ?
i guess ill never be certain i suppose, the only thing certain now is for whatever reason it has choosen me.

that voice . . . that beautiful voice. i believe her to be an angel, but she has only refures to her-self as Sorrow. ive actually begged and cried to her to take me from this broken world, she of few knows how lost and confused ive become here.

how perpetual depression has infected what is left of what used to resemble a heart.
she claims to hear the echoing of cries in the vast darkness of my soul.
i believe she knows where to find lanora and show me the way to neveah.

i fear now, that no GOD will ever take me. there have been countless times where i have reached outer neveah, im never to be worthy i am told.
i know sorrow can help me find the sanctuary seen only through visions and memories.

I MUST GET TO THE OTHER SIDE
I MUST FIND LANORA . . . . I PRAY FOR WINGS TO FLY.
PLEASE SORROW DONT LET ME FALL
BUT IF I DO, GIVE ME FLIGHT

II. it has been almost a year i believe since ive seen the hands of a clock. i refuse to let them control me anymore since that nightfall where they chased and forced me into hiding. i know it was HE that send them after me.
the gears that hide beneath his cold skin. the time manipulator is behind all this, i am certain.
because of him i have no awarness nor knowegle of the time or date. still unsure of what year it is; oblivious to all on the outside. id rather not know to be honest.
he's counting down my final hour . . . now only shelterd only by sounds of silence and the vast darkness.
mourge cold . . . afraid . . . still alone for now . . . in time lanora . . .

SOON.

entry III.(introduction to sorrow)

i can recall this certain memory. the very first time i heard her voice,
SORROW.
i was lanternless amongest the non living, running forever. the crackling below my feet . . . the sound of skull and bones breaking as i ran further into nothing. she was there, she guided me . . . she must of heard me.

THANK YOU FOR BEING THERE WHEN I NEEDED YOU.

(where are you now?)

ENTRY IV.

i saw a crying corpse before, she told me that she had been walking a niether world in search of a love to which had no name nor face. she went on to explain how she lost him to murder, i think.
i remember what she held in her hand was what appeared to once have been a half a mortal heart and that whom she seeked Possessed the other half.
i wished her luck on her uncertain quest and i traveled onward.

her cries could be heard in the distance like whispers in the wind.
the mile long trail of blood tears that followed like bread crums.
she'll never find him.
i must find my lanora soon though, nothing else matters.

I AM COMING BACK TO YOU LIKE I SAID I WOULD !

V.

the reflection of what once was is forever lost in another world;stolen by the hands of the majestic-the keeper of lost and unwanted souls.
if your soul roams a niether world and gets caught, it will be forever lost)
i cant be afraid, i must venture on.
I MUST FIND HER !
i just dont know how much longer i can hide. wait! i think i hear ticking
stay awake . . . .

i dont know whay i cant sleep. i wish to return to a dream capsule in which we were together.
if i were to be captured she would surely be erased.
there must be light somewhere around here.

entry

is capture my final stand . . . . their getting closer . . . i still dont know
how long ive been in hiding, honestly i don't know much of anything anymore.
all i know is her voice . . . . please someone make it stop . . . have to go,
i can hear ticking.

entry

does he really think he can stop me!? pushing me toward the edge will not break me . . . im still standing . . . i swore to her i wouldnt stop . . . i have and will continue to walk amongst the gates of hell and the outer relm untill my soul catches fire!

random night

tonight i was driving down the road of uncertainty . . . i saw what once was . . . . every time my eyes glanced at one of the mirrors its reflection showed only regrets and painful images of the past . . . one vision of impending sorrow . . . souls hiding from the majestic . . . others hiding from lies . . . and the truth . . . the dark tress that stood out in moonlight with cadavers rocking back and forth like wind-chimes . . . dozens already ive passed . . . sorrows voice instructs me to stop for no-one or nothing . . . to be cautious of demonic hitchikers . . . (she whispers) although she wont say how long i must drive for . . . but in the end it be clear . . . and if daylights not in sight . . . its not the end.

(same night continued)

i must STAY AWAKE . . . i didnt know how much longer i could keep driving . . . my eyes strained to keep from shutting out . . . up ahead i say what appeared to be one of many of the fallen angels . . . i coudn't stop . . . i was told i couldn't. the re-acurring sign that said
(SNOWISNOHERE)
was the last image i recall.

im sorry i have to stop . . . i cant continue . . . forgive me sorrow . . . this road seems never to end. where this road ends ill never be sure.

<u>ENTRY</u>

ah! once upon a time back in another life when my heart was whole,where we were two souls amongst the dark . . . where the snow covered the world and the trees where you rendered me powerless . . . . endless love with the conclusion uncertain . . . it was all i could of ever wanted . . . . but now without you,purposeless . . . trapped here for now . . . i miss you more than ever. i would gladly hand my soul to the majestic to feel you more last time . . . to hear you whisper into my heart "i love you"
haunted by your smile now only seen with closed eyes . . . a tormented soul . . . and a broken heart to comply. sometimes but only sometimes i should go back to where i thought it began . . . if i knew this mortal heart could endure such hurt . . . i would of torn it out then and there.

i keep asking is this even worth it . . . what is to become of me now . . . so unsure . . . why do i keep coming back to this sorrow forsaken torment . . . to revisit haunted memories . . . what if i dont find her . . . so many questions un-answered . . . . im losing control lanora, still no sign of you anywhere. perhaps the HYBRIDS were right . . . maybe i am marked by the majestic . . . what did i do to warrent this? did i have it coming? should i surrender now and hand over my soul to end this tedious nightmare . . . no! not yet my love . . . i made you a promise back in winter . . . i intend to keep it! what is left of my heart will continue until it completely devours . . . although it is stained in regret . . . you will always be my favorite.
i will search the outskirts of the departed . . . maybe your there . . .
(WISH ME LUCK SORROW)

ENTRY

did you hear that? you must of . . . the dead heard it . . . . i heard it . . . it
sounded like lanora . . . my mind has a sinster way of teasing my heart. the
cold whisper of a memory that showed a face never to forget . . . the ticking of
no clock in sight.
maybe i forgot how to sleep . . . well, i promise this . . . if i dont re-unite with
her in the forthcoming . . . the next time i do sleep will be my final. its almost
time to re-light the lantern and keep to my search.

i know if you or who ever is reading this must have an series of questions,
but that is for another time . . . in another tale . . . know that WINTER is the
last vague memory of what is left of salvation . . . there is rest and refuge that
is waiting to be rediscovered. this journey is yet to even see its start.
i can not even imagine the worst yet to come.
SOON . . . .

*"THEY ARE COMING! ETERNAL SLEEP AWAITS FOR THE WEAK OF
CAPTURE"*

come sorrow . . . there is much to be done.

MEMORY NUMBER—082107

STILL TILL THIS NIGHT I COULDNT BELIEVE THAT MEMORY WAS THE ONE OF FEW I SEARCHED FOR MY ENTIRE LIFE. I KNOW THAT YOU DIDNT KNOW ME . . . BUT I LOVED YOU ONCE UPON A DISTANT DREAM NOT OF THIS PLACE . . . PLEASE DONT BE SCARED, I HAVE WAITED MY ENTIRE LIFE FOR THIS WISH TO COME TRUE. NOTHING IN THIS WORLD OR THE NEXT WILL KEEP US APART. YOU HAVE MY HEART AND SOUL . . . I WILL GIVE MY-SELF UP TO REMIND YOU HOW YOU WERE THE ONLY MEMORY WHO COULD DRAG ME FROM WINTER AND BRING ME BACK TO LIFE FROM THE DARKEST ABYSS OF SORROW ONE LAST AND FINAL TIME.

NO OTHER COULD OF MADE ME WALK ACROSS THE ETERNITY OF MID AND HYLAND IN THE SNOW . . . AND I WOULD DO IT ALL AGAIN IF I MUST . . . JUST TO SEE YOU, THE ONLY ARENA FOR WHICH MY HEART NEEDED NO BATTLE NOR WAR . . .

NOW, YOUR MEMORY ONLY TO HAUNT IN THE FORM OF TRUTH AND "PERHAPS".

YOU WERE THE CLOSEST EASE WITH-OUT SLEEP I EVER HAD . . . SO FOR THAT . . . THANK YOU.

YOUR LOVE WILL CONTINUE MY QUEST . . . .

LOVE, YOU ALWAYS

08-21-07

"THIS TALE WILL BEGIN WITH THE WORDS OF REGRET, A BOYS JOURNEY THROUGH THE FLAMES AND THE FALL OF WINTER AND THE SEARCH FOR NAVEAH, THE HARDSHIPS THROUGH DEATH AND A PATH ALONE. CRYING FOR NO ONE TO HEAR;ENDURING YEARS OF A HOUSE BUT NEVER A HOME SPENDING EVERY WAKING HOUR IN FEAR OF HIS FATE AND THE ROAD TO THE WORLD OF THE UNKNOWN."

TWO SIDED MIRROR

my heart has shattered into countless pieces within the darkness of love . . .
the shadows of you that haunt my very soul. love so distinctive and vivid that
the void in my heart and mind will never to be completely filled. love seldom
only found by the few who believe in its reason, few have experienced and
have been fortunate to feel the magic while the tedious and abhorrent path of
lovers.

the potent affects of such beauty and love that contuses;tortures . . . .
agonizes.

*NOW IT SEEMS AS IF YOU WISH TO SLEEP TO ESCAPE THE
BRUTAL AND HARSH LONELINESS OF YOUR-SELF FABRICATED
REALITY WHERE YOU ARE INTOXICATED BY THE REFLECTIONS OF
IGNORANCE AND VACUOUS DECISIONS. HOPING TO HIBERNATE
FROM TEARS OF DISTANCE AND OVERCOME THE DEPTHS OF
ISOLATION OBLIVIOUSLY BLINDSIDED BY THE OVERWHELMING
REQUIEM OF YOUR PAST.*

(the time may come where the snow might not come to cover the world. and you will be faced with the clock)

WE ARE ALL BOUND BY A SHADOW WE CAN NOT FIND . . . . WE ALL HAVE A GHOST WE FEAR INSIDE.

WE ALL HAVE HAUNTING MEMORIES THAT DWELL WITHIN OUR MIND.

WE ALL HAVE A PAST FOR WHICH WE SEEM NEVER TO ESCAPE . . . . WE ALL CHASE THE THE UNCERTAIN PATH THAT determines OUR FATE.

I WILL ALWAYS HAVE THE WHOLE MISSING IN MY HEART THAT WHILE ALWAYS AND NEVER BE MINE.

STILL PRAYING FOR THE CHANCE TO SLEEP . . . THERE ARE OTHERS SOMEWHERE THAT SHARE THE SAME GRAVE AS I DO. THERE ARE OTHER ZOMBIES ROAMING LOST ON THIS SIDE WHO ARE EMPTY AND INCOMPLETE. STRAYS AMONGST THE ENDLESS STREETS STRANDED IN THE DREAMS UNABLE TO BE HERD OR SEEN.

"THE DAY WILL SOON APPROACH WHERE I CAN LEAVE MY PAST BEHIND, WHERE CHANGE WILL MAYBE WELCOME A NEW ME AND HEAL ALL THIS PAIN INSIDE . . . I WILL MAKE THE GRAVE SEE THAT IT REMAIN HOLLOW UNTILL FURTHER POINT IN TIME . . . HAVE A CHANCE AND LIFE I CAN FINALLY CALL MINE . . . IF YOU CAN JUST HOLD OUT LONG ENOUGH TO EDIFIY PERHAPS YOU AND I CAN JOURNY TOGETHER AS ONE BELOW TO THE OTHER-SIDE."

"WE WILL SEE WHAT BECOMES OF US IN THE END THAT GROWS NEAR . . . AN END THAT COMES FORTH DRAWING BLOOD FROM THE MORTALS THAT FEEDS FROM THE FEAR. THE ECHOES FROM HELL HAVE DEAFIN ME FOR THE LAST TIME . . . SO SHOW YOUR-SELF . . . YOU CANT HAVE HER . . . THIS SOUL IS MINE."

EVERYTHING HAS BEEN TAKEN FROM ME! THE MEMORY OF THE WORLD THAT NO LONGER IS STILL SEEMS AS VIVID AS I KNEW IT WOULD. THOSE TIMES ARE LOST AND GONE MY OLD FRIEND.SOON TO BE FORGOTTEN. AS THE DARKNESS SLOWLY BEGINS TO INFILTRATE MY HEART, MY MIND STRUGGLES TO REMAIN; FEAR AND TRUTH STARTS TO SINK IN.

NO MATTER HOW MUCH I WILL THOSE TIMES AND NIGHTS TO STAY, ONCE THIS LANTERN GOES OUT I KNOW INSIDE EVERYTHING WILL WITHER AWAY.

MY HOPE WILL ONLY LIVE ON IN THIS TALE WITHOUT END. AS LONG AS THE STRANGER AND THE THESE PAGES REMAIN, MY SOUL AND SORROW ARE NOW HERE AND ALWAYS TO STAY.

FORGIVE ME LANORA!
IF I EVER MAKE IT TO THE OTHER-SIDE I WILL SEEK YOU OUT AND WE SHALL AT LAST BE AS ONE YET AGAIN.

"the fallen sorrow of the mislead lovers who seek the answers from the night that will never see the start of another beginning, searching comfort of the soul to put hearts to ease. crying out to the unknown in hope of forgotten memories to finally seize . . . so perhaps at last they may finally see that only together from the dark be free; find the world and love they were ment to see . . . and maybe die together and become one as they were ment to be."

HOW DIFFERENT THE SKY HAS BECOME NOW, HOW IN A SINGLE MOMENT YOU WAIT FOR THE HEART TO PART . . . IM READY.

I CAN'T CONTINUE WITH YOU FROM HERE ON OUT . . . I MUST BATTLE ON ALONE. WISHING ON STARS THAT NO LONGER SHINE THE WAY FOR US WILL ONLY MAKE THIS HARDER.

THE MEMORIES YOU LET ME SHARE I SHALL ALWAYS HOLD TENDER UNTIL THE SLEEP OF ME . . . SOON WE'LL BE DEPARTED BY THE COURSE UNKNOWN . . . AND THE LINGERING HAUNT OF YOU WILL RESIDE WITHIN ALWAYS TO BE FOUND WHEN NEEDED.

I MUST NOW CRY THE TEARS I FEARED I NEVER WOULD . . . AS YOU GO ON WITH YOUR LIFE WITHOUT ME . . . JUST MY HEART AND OUR MEMORIES THAT I HOPE YOU KEEP WITH YOU NO MATTER WHERE YOU GO, AND KNOW THAT YOU WILL ALWAYS BE WITH ME . . . IN WINTER OR NOT.

IF YOU EVER WANT OUR SOULS TO RE-CONNECT AND OUR HEARTS TO MERGE AS THEY ONCE HAVE . . . . AND YOU WANT NOTHING ELSE . . . I SHALL ALWAYS BE IN THAT MEMORY WHERE WE FIRST KISSED . . . I WILL BE THERE READY TO RELIVE THE LOVE AND PAIN OF OUR MAGIC CAPSUEL . . . . I'LL BE WAITING.

GRAVE-DECISION

WHAT IF I NEVER ESCAPE THIS? ALL I FEAR AND HEAR IS THE SOUND OF ME SCREAMING INSIDE MY CASKET NEVER TO LEAVE MY BURIAL GROUND

ALL THE CORPSES IN LINE FORMATION . . . WALK AND WATCH AS THE SHADOWS CALL.
AS THE LIGHT DIMS TO WHERE THE VICTIMS CAN NEVER BEEN SEEN OR HEARD AT ALL.
I KNOW THAT WERE THE ONE THAT TOLD, IF WE FAIL TO ESCAPE THIS HELL THE MAJESTIC WILL SURELY KILL AND CAPTURE US BOTH. IVE TRIED TO TELL YOU ONCE UPON A VISION MANY ATTEMPTS AGO THAT RUNNING AND RELYING ON THE DARKNESS IS THE COWARDS KNOW. YOU DESERVE TO BE TORTURED AND HELD CAPTIVE SO THAT YOU WILL NEVER SEE LANORA AND NEVER RETURN HOME.

GRAVE-MISTAKE

"every tedious night as the restless father morns . . . in front of the hollow grave beneath him where the others have gone before. fearful of the moment that his secret will be told . . . a boy now lost to murder he must endure the other side, a side you dare not go. a chance to avenge your death and all the other spirits that will never becoming home.
you will pay and suffer for the childs life you stole . . . now go claim what was taken . . . go get back the life your owed!"

SOMEWHERE BETWEEN THE SLEEPLESSNESS AND THE REGRET, THE OVERWHELMING IMPRISONMENT HAS SEEM TO BE MORE TEDIOUS THAN EVER THOUGHT IMAGINED. I HAVE NO Strength NOR THE MIND AT THIS GATE TO KEEP MY SOUL ALIVE.

I STILL SEARCH . . . . I STILL HURT.

IS THERE ANY OTHER LIKE ME? NO SOUL, NO HEART . . . JUST THE TORMENT OF TIMES BEFORE.
THE GRAVE AWAITS TO CARRY AND TAKE ME FROM ONE HELL TO THE NEXT.
WHAT IS IT THAT I HAVE BEOME?

for what purpose is it to continue to live through out this place, i must face the truth that at the end of this we all must answer and can't ignore the whisper of death . . . . the fear of the unknown . . . . to die all alone. the fear of what lurks beyond our casket, to except our fate is the hardest endeavor and to to continue forever is the hope of most never to be carried out.

HOW COULD I DARE ASK ANOTHER TO EXCEPT MY MONSTER? TO ENDURE MY QUEST . . . TO ANSWER THE PAST. COULD I DO THAT? WOULD THEY EVER?

LOST IN GROUND: CRY ONE

**WILL NO ONE CATER TO MY CRIES? THIS WORLD AND MIND IS ON THE VERGE OF COLLAPSE;TIMES ARE WORSE THAN ANY BEFORE IT. SOON THE CRIES WILL BECOME MORE THAN JUST SUFFERING AND THE CLOCK WILL FREEZE.
NO ONE NOR LIVING NOR DEAD WILL SIEZE THE LAND THAT SOON WILL BE THE RUINS OF THE ONCE WAS.**

THE TEDIOUS STRUGGLE OF THE FORSAKEN IS NOW TO BECOME THE END OF US BOTH, THE END OF SEASONS;EVENTUALLY THE END OF TIMES. THE ENVIABLE DOOM THAT LURKS OUTSIDE THIS PLACE GROWS NEAR WITH EACH NIGHTFALL.

I BEG THAT SALVATION IS STILL SOMEWHERE TO BE FOUND,THAT SELF-DESTRUCTION NOT DICTATE THE VICTIMS THAT WILL GET BURIED INTO THE LOST-IN-GROUND.

THE TIME IS SOON TO FOLLOW . . . .

FOR-SHADOWING:CRY TWO

will any of the others see another way? the days are numbered for us.
prAy the ground does not give way.
in the last of words that i say, it always be the haunted epitaph that
resides on grave

"HERE LIES THE REMAINS OF THE ONLY HEAR AND SOUL NEVER
FROM DARKNESS TO FADE . . . A GHOST TO FAR GONE AND LOST TO
BE SAVED. ALWAYS IN HIDING;ALWAYS AFRAID
TILL THE NIGHT OF HIS LAST THAT MARKED THE WORDS
ON THIS GRAVE"

so long then forever my son . . . . perhaps we will have a chance to
battle again when my haunt here is finally done.

(PERHAPS)

THE ONLY FEAR THAT DWELLS NOW IS THE ONE WHERE I WAKE TO NEVER SEE YOUR FACE EVER AGAIN, THE ENTIRE WORLD WE CREATED IS ERASED FROM EXISTENCE. THE HEART WE ONCE SHARED SHATTERS LIKE THE GLASS ON OUR HOUR-GLASS

OUR MEMORIES AND LOVE FLOAT AND CARRY AWAY WITH THE WIND LIKE LEAVES IN THE FALL FROM A DISTANT PAST . . . LIKE A BEAUTIFUL TWILIGHT CASTED OUT FROM THE UNKNOWN BLINDING HEAVENS ABOVE THE WORLD BELOW . . . A HEAVEN THAT I DARE NOT HAVE ME . . . A HEAVEN I SHALL NOT GO ALONE.
OUR PLACE THAT WILL REMAIN THE SECRET THAT NO ONE BUT US WILL EVER KNOW.

I WILL PRAY TO THE DEAD THAT WE CAN ALWAYS STAY WITH
EACH-OTHER LOCKED INTO THIS PLACE.
I PRAY THAT BOTH OUR REMAINS AND SOULS CAN FIT IN ONE
CASKET, ONE HEART, ONE GRAVE.
SOMEWAY MY LOVE WILL BRING THIS TO HAPPEN ONE DAY.

THE ARROGANT **KISS OF THE MYSTIC SHADOW FROM THE PAST WILL BETRAY YOU I PROMISE**

"you showed me love that only few every find, you and i were destined from the beginning to share the world together; connected by fate and our souls never to break." IV

LIES OF THE SHADOWS

I ALWAYS THOUGHT THAT IF I COULD TRAP YOU, PULL YOU INTO MY
SHADOW FOR AT LEAST ONE MOMENT . . . THEN I COULD HOLD YOUR
MAGIC WITH ME FOREVER;THAT WOULD BE ENOUGH REASON. IT'S
BEEN A LONG WALK FROM WHERE I ONCE STARTED;STILL FURTHER
I WALK.

AFTER THIS PLACE IS GONE LIKE EVERYTHING THING ELSE . . . THEN
WHAT? YOU WILL RETURN TO THE VERY PLACE THIS ALL BEGAN,
AND YOU WILL RETURN TO THESE PAGES AND ENDURE THE DEMON
THAT LIVES WITHIN THE HEART YOU TRUELY DONT BELIEVE IN
ANYMORE. I KNOW HOW MUCH IT HURTS . . . I KNOW THE PAIN YOU
HIDE DEEP INSIDE YOUR GHOST . . . . IT WILL ALWAYS REMAIN UNTIL
YOU CAN FIND THE WAY TO LET GO OF THE PAST.

I KNOW ITS BEEN MANY YEARS SINCE THE SHADOWS LIED; YET IT
FEELS AS IF ONLY IN A INSTANT.
THE NIGHTS HAVE COME AND GONE AND YOU ARE STILL HERE,
YOUR STILL IN PAIN.
THE BEAUTIFUL SKY THAT ONCE WAS SHARED WITH THOSE NO
LONGER PRESENT IS NOW THE REFLECTION OF DREAMS THAT WILL
FALL WITH THE STARS OF DISAPPOINTMENT.

I ONCE ROAMED THESE VERY GRAVES IN SEARCH OF MY OWN
GHOST, ONLY TO FIND THAT THE GHOST NO LONGER HAUNTED, TO
LEARN THAT IF I WERE TO FIND REST I WOULD HAVE TO REVISIT THE
ORIGINS OF MY DEATH; MY CURSE.

THAT THE TEARS WOULD NEVER STOP, THE HOLE IN MY SOUL
WOULD NEVER BE FIXED.

THAT NO MATTER HOW LONG I LIVED HERE ALONE, YOUR MAGIC WAS
ALWAYS SOMEWHERE TO BE FOUND; IT WAS THAT VERY GIFT THAT
HAS KEPT GOING THUS FAR.

(MEMEORY RELAPSE)

"I HAVE BETRAYED MY OWN FOR THE SAKE OF THE LOST. CURSE ME TO THE DEPTHS BELOW SO I MAY KNOW THE STRUGGLE THAT THE OTHERS KNOW . . . . I SHOULD OF TORN OUT THIS SHAPE INSIDE LONG BEFORE THIS TIME. FORGIVE ME!"

THE PRISON THEY CHOOSE FOR ME SEEMS ALL BUT TO COMFORTABLE NOW . . . .

THE OTHER-SIDE ISNT TO FAR OR NEAR, THE FREEDOM AND LOVE I SEEK WILL SADLY NEVER APPEAR.

IF NO ONE SHALL HELP OR BELIEVE THE WORDS I SPEAK, MAY HE CAPTURE AND DEVOUR THE MINDS AND SOULS OF THE NON-

BELIEVERS AND THE WEAK. MY CHANCE WAS VANISHED LONG AGO . . . EVEN WITH ESCAPE I HAVE NO WHERE LEFT TO GO AND

NOTHING BUT ETERNAL TORMENT TO SHOW.

COUNTLESS NIGHTS HERE;TRAPPED FOREVER.

THE FROZEN CLOCK THAT MAY NEVER BE FIXED . . .

I DARE NOT ASK ANY OTHER TO SHARE THE CLOCK WITH ME THAT CANT BE REPAIRED.

IN THIS TOWN WHERE THE NIGHTS SEEM TO NEVER-END AND MY WILL TO CONTINUE SLOWLY BEGINS TO BEND BECAUSE YOU

REALIZE HERE YOU TRUELY BECOME ALONE AND YOU NEVER HAVE FAMILY OR FRIENDS. WHERE IN EVEN IN DEATH YOU SHALL

NEVER BREAK APART;NEVER WITNESS AN END OR A START. SEARCH ALL ETERNITY FOR THE REST OF YOUR SOUL IN HOPES ONE

NIGHT YOU MAYBE ABLE TO DISCOVER AND REPAIR THE MISSING PIECES OF THE LONG FORGOTTEN HEART. VENTURE ONWARD.

FIND THE WILL AND THE MUST NO MATTER THE COST, OTHERWISE BE DOOMED TO BECOME ONE OF THE LOST.

i wonder whatever became of that blinded corpse on the outskirts, perhaps the death row toll got to them all . . . what do you think? never the less all our nights are numbered i suppose . . . . i need to try and focus . . . remember something, anything . . . . or close your eyes and bring it all to the END. i fear when the time finally arrives i may forget, this is harder than i could ever of fathomed.

love over dark . . . regret over all.

1-all i ever asked for was just a chance to see what they see, to have what they have . . . to live without this.
to what it would feel like to wake up again, to where we all were together with nothing in the way of our fate. i miss it so much sorrow . . . i don't want to cry anymore . . . i don't want to feel like this! why me? i know i said i wouldn't ask but its not fair, why us? i didn't deserve this anymore than anyone else ever has.

"i know she would do the same, she looked beyond the corpse and saw in me what no other could see; beyond the curse to help through the suffering to finally let go of this ghost and find what i have been in search for the person i wanted to be."—IV

2-The hardship of enduring many faces of death, abandonment the only one true friend. I know there are others like me . . . others without hope, without result; A life-time of enduring a house but never a home.

its hard to imagine the time that once was in a world that no longer is;as the clock counts down to my last and final moment in this nightmare never ending, the tales of the many paths that have brought me to this place seem as distant as the world from which they were conceived.

countless pain and suffering follow by (the) tragic tears of a soul lost amongst the living and forgotten. afraid of the change of tides, always haunted by ghosts of the past, and secrets told only in silence.
born into darkness to forever be held captive, trapt seeking freedom from torment. dwelling on memories that continue to repete and destroy the will instead of liberating.

hollow and alone with only the whispers of the wind from the voice of the sorrow, without the comfort of friends or family.

WAITING FOR A NIGHT THAT WILL NEVER SEE AN END AND NOR SEE A TOMORROW.

NO OTHERS WILL EVER SEE WHAT THE EYES OF THE FORSAKEN SEE no mortal nor hybrid could ever be as lost and chapfallen as the ones who dream without sleep the unseen hiding to escape from the truth that will always find. the unheard screaming of the victims that deception abandons and leaves behind.

the shadows will only provide you cover for so long, untill the light catches up with you and the stronghold is no more.

prepare your-self for the coming unknown, as the story slowly unfolds with your heart still not working from a reality sub-zero cold.

THE CHILD YOU ONCE LEFT BEHIND HAS NOW BECOME THE MONSTER THAT HAS LOSS MORE THAN THE WILL TO CONTINUE IN THIS LAND OF RUINS. HIDDEN DEEP INSIDE THE CHAMBER OF TORTURE LIES A HEART CONFINED TO THE ABYSS OF A BROKEN WORILD.

THE STRUGGLE THAT HAS SEEMED TO BE SET IN GRAVESTONE; EVENTUALLY LEAD TO THE ROAD THAT WILL ONLY EVER BE WALKED ON BY ONE. THE CRIMSON PATH THAT FEW EVER DARE NOT GO. A CHILDS FATE NEVER TO BE KNOWN. A GHOST OF A STRANGER FEARED TO FOREVER ROAM ALONE.

please try to forgive me! the battle within still continues . . . this demon trapped inside for as long as the sky showed stars has yet to capture and torture another.
the wrath of the impending rage that manipulates the darken heart of the unworthy, i fear its slowly closing in to conclude my fate as a forgotten ghost of a world that will no longer be.
the reflection of a life that will never be mine . . . heart and the love of another will never be given.
afraid of the sorrow;afraid of tomorrow, will my mind last long enough to witness tomorrow . . . or will all these demons remain till death do me justice and my casket is lowered below to be forever forgotten.

I PROMISE YOU I WILL TRY TO FIND MY WAY

ETERNAL WAR: DARK VOID 1

if you truley believe that love isnt real just because its a product of your
own perception, that doesnt make it true sorrow.
everything is a product of my perception . . . if love isnt real . . . then
perhaps nothing is real . . . . accept this all . . . or accept nothing. Either
way mind heart knows her to be real as snow, as beautiful as the sky . . .
my heart wont lie to me anymore and my mind not deceive me.

"I WANT MORE. YEARS IT'S BEEN SINCE I'VE BEEN TRUELY HAPPY,
SINCE THE ICE CLEAR SKY WAS BRIGHT ENOUGH TO SHINE UPON
THE WORLD ONCE BUILT ON THE REFLECTION OF VISIONS OF A LIFE
ONCE LIVED. I STILL TILL THIS MOMENT CRY MY-SELF TO WAKE AND
SLEEP . . . I SCREAM DEEP INTO THE DARKNESS OF MY ENTERNAL
VOID BEGING FOR SOMETHING TO BRING CHANGE TO THIS CRUEL
EXISTENCE FOR WHICH I FEAR WILL NEVER HAVE AN END. LIKE
WAKING FROM AN ESCAPE IN HORROR, NOT BECAUSE THE DREAM
AND VISION WAS OVER, BUT BECAUSE MY HEART KNEW IT WAS
AND WILL ALWAYS BE JUST THAT; MAYBE I WAS THE FORSAKEN,
MAYBE THIS WAS THE WAY MY WORLD HAD TO BE FOR WHAT—EVER
REASON . . . I WAS MENT TO BATTLE THIS ENTERNAL WAR WITHIN . . .
THAT FROM THE ACCIDENT OF BIRTH I WOULD BE MARKED FOR
DEPRESSION THAT FLOWED THROUGH MY BODY . . . THE ANGEL OF
WRATH THAT SPAWNED THE DEMON IN WHICH MY HEART WOULD
SEE NO MERCY, FEEL NO RELIEF. WHAT MADE THE OTHERS SO MUCH
MORE WORTHY? SURELY I CAN'T BE THE ONLY ONE TRAPPED IN THIS
GRAVE . . . TRAPPED ALONE. IS IT TOO LATE AT THIS POINT? MUST I
SUFFER FOR THE CREATION NEVER MENT TO BE, MUST THE DARK
WITHIN ME BE THE ONLY SHADOW EVERYONE ELSE EVER SEES . . . IS
THERE ANYHTING ELSE BEYOND WHAT I HAVE ENDURED SINCE THE
START; WHILE THIS WAR RIPS ME APART OTHER SOULS AMONGST
ME CARRY ON WITHOUT ANY KNOWELGE OF THIS OTHER-SIDE NOR
THE WAR BEING FOUGHT."—IV

"REMEMBER THE LOVE THAT TURNED THE WORLD WHITE, AS IT
DESENDED FROM THE SKY ABOVE TO COVER THE LAND WHEN THE
REFLECTION WAS BRIGHT. SOON YOU WILL NO LONGER REMEMBER
AND YOU WILL SURELY FORGET THE REASON FOR WINTER AND THE
PURPOSE IT MENT. YOU'LL FORGET ALL THAT IS LOST AND ALL THAT
HAS WENT.

ONCE THE DARK TAKES OVER, TO THE FLOORS OF HELL BELOW YOU SHALL BE SENT"—?

all still seems lost sorrow . . . ghost of a complete stranger, the mirror image of the world i will never have, never worthy of . . . this void in my soul all in sake of her . . . i feel trapped in the nightmare of that stranger . . . ghost of a soul with no reason . . . inner strength is deteriorating quickly like the sand of an hourglass.

SNOW ANGEL: MEMORY ONE

COME WITH ME TO THE PLACE THAT WILL KEEP YOU AWAY FROM PAIN . . . FEAR NOT OF THE WORLD WHERE YOUR FUTURE UNFOLDS. DO WHAT YOU HAVE BEEN ASKED, DO WHAT YOU HAVE BEEN TOLD. OR BEFORE YOU KNOW IT THE SKY WILL COME FALLING AND STRAIGHT TO THE MAJESTIC YOU SHALL GO NEVER TO SEE MOONLIGHT AND NEVER FEEL SNOW. A PRISON SO DARK . . . AND YOU WILL HAVE VENTURED AND NOTHING TO SHOW.

ONCE I WALKED TILL DAWN IN THE COLD BACK IN MEMORY WITH HOPE THAT I WILL SEE YOUR FACE AND STEAL YOUR HEART AS YOU ONCE DID MINE. HOLD IT CLOSE WITH CARE AND PROTECT YOUR SOUL FROM THE MAJESTIC BELOW.
THE COUNTLESS MILES DOWN ROADS I DIDNT KNOW, WITH NOTHING BUT ICE, FROZEN, WITH AN ENDLESS JOURNEY TO GO.
MY ONLY TRUE REASON . . . .

WILL YOUR KISS KEEP ME LEVEL? WILL IT KEEP MY MIND STABLE, WILL IT GIVE ME THE STRENGTH TO MAKE ME WILLING AND ABLE?

I SWEAR TO YOU I WILL WALK THROUGH THE DARK AND THE FEAR IN HOPE THAT THOSE FEELINGS WE ONCE SHARED WILL NOT DISAPPEAR WHEN THE NIGHTS OVER, KNOWING THAT NO MATTER WHAT I DID WHAT I HAD TO BE THERE MY DEAR.

THE SECRET SERAPHIM

the deplorable tears of the illogical angel has scathe the sinlessness of my heart . . . the abrasive behavior has tormented the sprightiness among the remains of the cadavor, the subsist within the realms of reality . . . the deafing cries echo through out the shattered earth causing tragic floods that demolish hopes and dreams that were once reinforced by lanterns that would refulgence . . . surrounded by eternal anguish and darkness praying for light to give way. the tears wasted on otiose and enviable hurt . . . when the Gods agazed the gates and conveyed you from the heavens and placed you here . . . they knew you were uncomparable to any before. aesthetical angel never to be down-hearted, portentous to every soul, every hybrid and mortal.

A HEART, HAS SHATTERED INTO PIECES IN THE ESSANCE OF LOVE . . . THE SHADOW THAT WONT LEAVE My SOUL BE . . . A SHADOW SO DISTINCTIVE AND VIVID THAT THE VOID IN MY SOUL WILL NEVER BE FILLED. LOVE ONLY SELDOM FOUND ON THE ABHORRENT PATH OF THEIR LIFE. THE EFFECTS OF YOUR LOVE AND BEAUTY SO POTENT THAT IT CONTUSES AND FORCES SLEEP TO ESCAPE THE BRUTAL AND HARSH LONLYNESS OF MY SELF-FABRICATED REALITY WHERE INTOXICATED BY THE REFLECTIONS OF IGNORANCE AND VACUOUS DECISIONS AND MEMORIES. WANTING TO HIBERNATE FROM THE PAST.

that sign i mentioned to you earlier in the memory . . . do you remember it? "SNOWISNOWHERE"

this is the part where the memory splits . . . if you saw SNOW-IS-NO-WHERE then you have not followed me through winter. you still have time . . . hope is still with you! and you can turn back now.

but . . . if you saw what i saw . . . SNOW-IS-NOW-HERE then your too far gone im afraid. DO NOT READ ONWARD! do not follow me ! it will only end in pain and regret.

the path is yours to venture . . . . BUT should you choose to carry onward, know there will never be any chance of returning.

so . . . before you turn this page . . . just remember what i've told you.

what lies ahead is the one memory left that replays in the vortex between my mind and the heart of sleep . . . forever to be the distant echo in the haunt of my past . . . .

WARLOCK OF SALEM

a spirit from distant time followed the hurt to the trials where the murder of innocents swept the land like a plague of ignorance . . . the warlock of salem that stole the life and souls from the women and children as for-seen in a vision once seen in the fall of man.
dragging the bodies through and across the ground of once was, is now no longer the stronghold of purity.

i believe that this capsuel is where our souls first encountered and concealed our love through tears and tragedies;through ropes and flames that hung your soul for all to see . . .

could salem be where the origin of my evil and first sin? i know as you hung there swinging in the wind that one day we would be together in another time and life . . . that within murder came salvation . . . that your murder was the first of haunts to come . . . when i find you i shall beg for your forgiveness . . . one day you will see it was the only way we could be together . . . that life dare not have us, the next one will bring us together.

if your soul is still captive there, i promise i will release it upon arrival my love . . . cut you down from the gallows and return you to the present.
to our world where the snow not melt . . . where the magic we shared and the love we felt will forever stay in our hearts . . .

"AS I LOOKED OVER THE EDGE AT THE LIFE AND WORLD I NEVER HAD . . . . I KNEW, I DIDN'T BELONG;THAT I WAS APART OF SOMETHING NOT ALL BELOW WOULD ACCEPT OR UNDERSTAND . . .
THE DEMONIC SHERPA THAT ONCE LEAD ME TO THE TOP OF MT. MISERY WOULD SOON GUIDE ME TO THE TOP OF ANOTHER MOUNTAIN BEYOND THE GATES OF SLEEP. THE EVIL THAT DWELLED WITHIN THE RELM OF THE REGRET WOULD SOON RELEASE THE SECRETS MY PAST COULD NO LONGER KEEP"

THE SCREAMING ECHOS IN SILENCE . . . . AND YET STILL THE DEAFENING TORMENT THAT I HEAR SADDLY AS GROWN TO BE ONLY THE FRIEND IVE COME TO KNOW IN HERE . . . .

STILL AWAKE TO FIGHT SLEEP TILL THE PEICES MEND SO THIS JOURNEY CAN FIND THE END WITHOUT THE HELP OF KNOWING SURRENDER AGAIN . . . I WILL THIS TIME ONLY PRAY TO A HEAVEN . . . . WILL A HYBRID-ANGEL YOU CARE TO SEND?

"I FEAR THAT MY MND START TO SPLIT AND MY WILL STARTS TO BEND . . . THAT THE ONLY SALVATION IS TO DEPEND ON THIS PEN TO WALK ME ACROSS ANOTHER HELL IN SEARCH OF THE END."

YOU'VE ALWAYS SEEM TO RE-LIVE THE PAST IN A SINGLE NIGHT . . . YOU ALWAYS SEEM TO HURT IN YOUR OWN WAY. ONCE THE SHADOWS LIED . . . THE MEMORIES RESIDE.
I CAN NO LONGER LET YOU BEG ME TO FREE YOU . . . ALL YOU DO IS HIDE . . . ONCE ITS TIME TO LET GO . . . YOU AND SORROW WILL KNOW THAT IT ALL BELONGS TO ME.

although you weren't always here, you were always felt . . . . our fate shall cross ways once again when the time comes to finally say good-bye to our creators and find the world where its safe and calm . . . where the relm of sleep is the final resting of our minds and hearts.

(separation parted us . . . salvation will connect us once again i promise you)

i never thought that this was the way of our future, i always visioned our life free of the sins of the outside . . . where our love could be alive and held for all eternity until one of us decided different. it murders my heart to see the way others turned out, if only i had the power to save all and my-self from the hurt and the pain for which they do not merit.

SOMETIMES I GET SAD KNOWING THAT THE LIFE OUT THERE CONTINUED WITHOUT ME . . . THAT THE WORLD MOVED FOWARD AND LEFT ME BEHIND TO FIGHT THIS ALONE . . . . THE TEARS HAVE ALREADY

FALLEN DEEP WITHIN THE ABYSS OF MY SORROWS . . . LIKE DARK CLOUDS FLOATING OVER MEMORY.

IT'S NOT MUCH LONGER NOW . . . SOON THERE WILL BE NO MORE PAGES TO CONFIDE IN; NOTHING TO TRAP THE HURT.

THE HOLLOW VASTNESS OF MY HEART WITH SOON BE AS MY PAST IS NOW . . .

I HOPE NONE OF YOU EVER FEEL THIS . . .

STILL CHAPFALLEN? NOW THAT THIS PLACE IS ALMOST GONE, THE CHAPTER OF AN END TO BEGIN ANOTHER. TELL ME WHAT SHADOWS STILL DWELL, IS IT THE DEATH OF A LONG LOST LOVER? OR MAYBE THE FORGOTTEN GHOST OF YOUR NO NAME MOTHER. I CANT PROMISE THE NEED FOR FEAR WILL BE NO MORE, THE FORSAKEN MAY NOT POSSESS THE KEY TO OPEN THE DOOR TO YOUR OLD MEMORIES OR ANSWERS THAT YOU HAVE BEEING SEARCHING FOR.

I STILL CAN NOT FATHOM THE DESIRE OF YOUR WILL TO ESCAPE. WE WILL SEE IF IN THE PRETENSE OF YOUR QUEST FOR FATE THAT THIS DREAM COULD BECOME THE PROSPECT AND CREATION OF YOUR MAKE

I DO REMEMBER THE WAY THE WIND WOLD SOFTLY WHISPER WALKING DOWN THE ROAD OF UNCERTAINTY THAT MAGIC OF THE BEAUTIFUL SIGHT OF ALL THE COLORS OF BROKEN EARTH FALLING FROM ABOVE AS MY FEET STEPPED ON CHANGE.
A POTENT SMELL SO FAMILIAR . . . BRINGING BACK LONG LOST THOUGHTS LOST IN A FABRICATED CAPSULE STOLEN AND HELD PRISONER IN TIME.
IVE TRIED COUNTLESS TIMES TO FIND IT AGAIN, IVE SEARCHED FAR AND WIDE WITH NO TRACE.

THE SOFT WHISPER OF THE WIND SAYING
(LET GO)

I HOPE THAT WHEN SHE PASSES OVER, HER SOUL IS HELD CAPTIVE FOREVER IN A STATE OF TORMENT. THE AFTER LINGERING HAS NO ROOM FOR MURDERS . . . SHE TOOK ALMOST EVERY SINGLE FRAGMENT OF HOPE I EVER HAD . . . SHE WAS A PURE VILLAIN OF WHICH HAD NEVER BEEN DISCOVERED BEFORE NOR AFTER.

SHE KEPT MY HEART LOCKED AWAY WITHIN A PRISON BUILT OF SHADOWS THAT WAS GUARDED FOR WHICH THERE WAS NO ENTRY . . . I WILL NEVER RETURN TO ANY OF THOSE MEMORIES EVER AGAIN. I SHALL LET HER HANG THERE FOR ALL TO SEE BEFORE THE HORROR SHE CREATED.

IT WAS NOT HER PLACE TO TAKE THE LIFE OF THE CHILD NOT BORN . . . SHE WILL HAVE TO LIVE WITH THAT CONTINUING NIGHTMARE AS SHE PAYS FOR HER SINISTER SINS SHE CARES NOT OF.

SHE WILL ONLY REMAIN HERE WITHIN THIS PAGE . . . AND NEVER TO ESCAPE HER PUNISHMENT, WITHOUT COMFORT OF WAKING.

YOU DESERVE EVERY OUNCE OF SUFFERING YOU ENDURE AS ONCE HAVE I . . . . SO LONG.

I. HOLLOW VASTNESS: PART 1

since she departed, my world along with my heart became a vast hollow prison for which there would be no escaping. trapped and held captive till times end . . . bound to roam searching for answers to questions that never mattered,pretending that i could teach and train my mind to let another take control . . . spending a life-time within a dream knowing never to wake. crying forever into the tides of the forgotten in hopes she might return and shelter me from perpetual lost . . . all in vein . . . my soul will never be found . . . never find salvation . . . never laid to rest.

2. HOLLOW VASTNESS: IMAGINATION OF THE WICKED

i once followed the demonic sherpa through the imagination of the evil and wicked . . . to the top of the mountain of remorse where i was in search of nevaeh.
i vividly remember the trail of corpses that lead the way and stopped mid-way, the visible snow that laid on top where the fail of the lost laid across the land like cold and deep ocean of regret. although years have been taken since the clock began . . . the state for which it left me was unlike any-other. when i reached the top the reflection from below was blinding the world in front of me . . . and it was that moment i knew it was only the beginning im afraid . . . .

"GHOST OF A STRANGER"
(part 1)

IF ONLY A SINGLE KISS COULD MAKE ME MISS THE SMILE YOU ONCE HAD . . . . WHAT KIND OF PURPOSE WOULD I ENDURE IF YOUR GONE?

NIGHTMARES ARE APPARENT, IF I SLEEP WILL MY PAST SECRETS KEEP.

how could i ever forgive the lies of the one that choose to leave me alone below with hurt and nothing but tears and cry, paralyzed but the eyes of another time. tears of torture that flood my emptiness, the broken heart and lonely ghost is all to be left of this.
the presence of what is no longer certain, the haunt that refuses to abandon the stronghold where i once held your heart ever so close to mine; each second with you seemed to be a gift from nevaeh forever to be frozen in time.
you had me believe you were an angel like no other, now to rewind and relive is a path still unsure . . . to forgive and forget is one burden i will bare for you no more my dear . . . only one of us will witness the fall and ruins with the close of this door.

it was for-told that this love was never strong enough to cater the mind of the forsaken or the lost; the torment of a life without your heart.
the perpetual depression that dwells and screams with every captured soul by the hands of the one who roams the vast dark below.
love forever gone and forgotten like ashes traveling in distant wind always to float amongst the broken and shattered hybrid hearts with only shadows of regret to ease the pain of atrophy.

I REFUSE TO STAND BY THIS LIFE WHILE YOU SEARCH FOR SKY ONE LAST TIME. I PROMISE IT SHALL BE YOU, NOT I THAT COWARDS AND HIDES IN A SELF-MADE GRAVE OF CRIES . . . . MAKE YOUR AMENDS . . . PREPARE FOR THE LAST AND FINAL CRY . . . YOUR FINAL GOOD-BYE.

FREE-HOLD

it's been so long since i saw you last, it seems like only the other moment you took me in and saved me from the torment. i hope you know how much your love did for me when i needed it most, i always wish i could just go back and stay longer, that time wasn't meant for me . . . but know that everything around me now reminds me of what we shared;until i go, your memory is always inside.

your presence is always felt;your image was the last reflection i'd ever see of her . . . through you she was still there . . . still even in death showing the love that was always to be. know that because of you my soul was released and free within the world we shared.

it still brings tears to my face knowing neither of you are here now, but i know in my heart one day, no matter what side, we will find each-other and tell you everything i had to endure with-out you.

i pray one day i will awake to find this was all just the nightmare i continue to endure . . . that somewhere i am happy . . . at ease. that i have a home to return to, a family waiting for me there ready to welcome me back from the hell from which i have been.

where the world is as beautiful as i remember it once was, to look out upon the world and see the living instead of the dead. to awake never to see the corpse in the mirror . . . or listen to the whispers of sorrow . . . . maybe return to the ocean and look out on the lights in the distance that seemed impossible to reach.

what you are about to endure was a path once taken by my-self long ago. what i can tell you is it be nothing like you have ever had to face . . . that your will and strength will be tested till you feel like your heart and soul have nothing left. i cant tell you why it has chosen you or any of us . . . once we are marked, there is no going back . . . just forward. the suffering will come to you and will consume you.

its ok to fear the unknowing . . . . this battle will not be easy . . .

the journey will seem to never end, but let me tell you that the pain is not the worst . . . the worst would be to surrender to the nightmare.

unlike me . . . you have purpose . . . Reason. my curse will always be the answer am afraid i may never get.

you have all the advantages i never had . . . i know you can overcome this . . . .

CORPSE IN THE SNOW: PART 1

As your hidden below, the hollow world where the souls of the dead are forced to go . . . i will always remember the way you were back then, when the road ahead was nothing but white.

im so sorry i left you behind my love. every time the sky comes falling i still search this land in hopes that your still some where in there waiting for my return.

maybe once again we can walk along-side the clouds on the ground of that snow covered town bound deep within the sounds of age, buried below somewhere waiting to be found once again so that we can roam the land as we once have together until the night ends and we are never to see one another ever again.
if i chose to return things will be different next memory around.

when the wind comes back to haunt me me . . . i still feel you

i dont know if anyone or thing can ever control my being as you once have and hopefully always will.

you know no other before nor after could ever make me feel the embrace of true love like only you could.

to us the snow fell forever . . . to share that with any other is a sin i could never . . . .

forgive me for this WRONG that has separated our eternal magic . . . and shattered our doubt

ONE NIGHt SOON . . . . I PROMISE . . .

CORPSE IN THE SNOW: RELAPSE TO REASON

all those days are gone for now! her and only her could of made the visions of my world. i know you are still there waiting alone in the quietness of the winter.
the dream was always meant for us to lose . . . that memory was buried with reason with the fall of your season . . . maybe you can salvage it in a distant day . . . someway. maybe somewhere both of your souls you once shared are still together walking in the silence of the snow . . . WAITING FOR YOU. did you ever truely leave? the haunting question that still bares no answer . . . so walk in the endless snow till love do you justice because once i find you both, you will forget all the memories and the love that you felt . . . once your captured and gone you will sieze to remember the love surely after the snow and love start to melt. like romeo who is haunted by the shadow of juliet, her ghost still falls from the balcony of time . . . will you wait forever? scared to live alone . . . afraid to die together. the zeitgeist of your past is the catalysis that triggered this travesty . . . soon i will but this to its end. stop chasing the able and the no longer is . . . i know the deception that is within the nightmares always to re-surface . . . running will only tire . . . embrace the depths of the abyss that conjuror your curse.

i my-self once ventured beyond the the burning dimension of forgiveness to awake from the shadows of the corpses that slept within . . . the gates between secured by of which i can not say . . . the burning of souls of the so called innocent to cleanse the wicked of sin and to erase memory.

iii.

since time began, your brutal vengeance for another has tore us apart and forced us into separation from our memories. blood scattered through out the land never to reunite till the demon inside could finally leave. now after all this . . . your end will be a sad burden on us all, the comfort we thought would never find has come when the time is almost done; your soul on the verge of crossing. know that even in our darkest battle i knew one day you would come to realize the wrong in hopes you would make it right before it was too late.

the demon that spent a life time consuming you is now my burden within . . . afraid that i will suffer the same fate and end up in the place we all feared; even though you don't have much time here . . . i want you to know that i do love you.

WINTERS REMNANT: THE DARK LURK

I, LIKE FEW OTHERS BARE THE FEELING OF LIVING WITH PAIN WITHIN . . .
ALWAYS HURTING . . . ALWAYS SUFFERING.
IT GETS SO OVERWHELMING THAT THE WORLD OUTSIDE SEEMS TO
SLOWLY FADE AWAY WITH EACH PASSING SECOND, THEY WILL NEVER
FULLY UNDERSTAND WHAT IT FEELS LIKE TO CARRY ON LIKE THIS . . .
I'D SAY LIVING . . . BUT THAT'S NOT REALLY WHAT WE DO . . . LIVING
IS SOMETHING I'VE NEVER HAD THE JOY OF DOING . . . SURVIVING
AND TRYING TO FIGHT THE GHOST OF DEPRESSION IS NOT MY IDLE
WAY OF "LIVING". WHEN THE TIMES OF THE ONCE WERE NO LONGER
IS, ALL I EVER TRUELY WANTED WAS A FAMILY. TO HAVE A TANGIBLE
SANCTUARY . . . RATHER THAN THE FABRICATED REALITY I'VE COME
TO CREATE THROUGH DREAMS AND VISIONS.

I'VE HEARD "THINGS CAN BE WORSE" BUT BY HOW MUCH . . . WHY CAN'T
THEY BE BETTER? THOSE WHO DON'T HAVE WHAT I DO WILL NEVER
BE ABLE TO FATHOM THE DARK LURK OF PERPETUAL SORROW THAT
HAS FOREVER BEEN CASTED BY SHADOWS OF THE WORLD BEFORE.
HAVING NO ONE TO HELP YOU THROUGH THE VAST AND TEDIOUS
PATHS OF THE UNKNOWING . . . TO AWAKE IN DARKNESS KNOWING
NOTHING AND NO-ONE IS THERE WITHIN.

NEVER KNOW WHAT'S LIKE DOWN HERE WHEN ALL YOU HAVE IS THE
SILENCE AND THE HAUNTING GHOSTS OF YOUR PAST TO KEEP YOU
FROM TRAVELING TO A DREAM CAPSUEL WHERE PERHAPS YOU CAN
SALVAGE REFUGE.

WHAT I WOULDN'T GIVE TO RETURN TO THE ONE MEMORY I'VE KEEP
THROUGH ALL THIS . . . THE ONE PLACE WHERE I REMEMBER THE
FEELING OF LOVE . . . AND MY HEART WAS STRONGER THAN IT'S
EVER BEEN . . . WHERE THE SLEEPLESSNESS WAS NOT FROM A WAR
WITHIN . . . BUT TO WATCH THE SUNRISE OVER THE WORLD AS IF IT
WAS THE VERY FIRST SIGHT OF LIFE . . . IT ALMOST SEEMED WORTH
EVERY DREAMLESS NIGHT.

BUT NOW, IT'S BECOME SO UNRULY BEING IN THIS PLACE . . . NO
MATTER HOW HARD I CRY . . . AND NO MATTER HOW HARD I FIGHT
THE OTHER INSIDE . . . MY MIND IS SLOWLY SLIPPING FURTHER AND
FURTHER FROM FOCUS. I AM SO SCARED THAT ONCE MY MIND AND
MEMORY SPLIT AND SHATTER, THERE WILL BE NOTHING LEFT OF
WINTER . . . NOTHING LEFT OF MY SOUL . . . IN WHICH IT WILL BECOME AS

EMPTY AND HOLLOW AS MY HEART IS NOW . . . I FEAR I AM ETERNALLY DRAINED FROM TRYING TO FIGHT FOR SO LONG.

TO CONTINUE THIS WAR WILL ONLY END IN FAILURE . . . JUST AS WAS MY QUEST FOR A MIRACLE DID.

EVERYTHING HAS BEEN TAKEN FROM ME! THE MEMORY OF THE WORLD THAT NO LONGER IS STILL SEEMS AS VIVID AS I KNEW IT WOULD. THOSE TIMES ARE LOST AND GONE MY OLD FRIEND . . . SOON TO BE FORGOTTEN. AS THE DARKNESS SLOWLY BEGINS TO INFILTRATE MY HEART, MY MIND STRUGGLES TO REMAIN; FEAR AND TRUTH STARTS TO SINK IN.

NO MATTER HOW MUCH I WILL THOSE TIMES AND NIGHTS TO STAY, ONCE THIS LANTERN GOES OUT I KNOW INSIDE EVERYTHING WILL WITHER AWAY.

MY HOPE WILL ONLY LIVE ON IN THIS TALE WITHOUT END. AS LONG AS THE STRANGER AND THE THESE PAGES REMAIN, MY SOUL AND SORROW ARE NOW HERE AND ALWAYS TO STAY.

FORGIVE ME LANORA!
IF I EVER MAKE IT TO THE OTHER-SIDE I WILL SEEK YOU OUT AND WE SHALL AT LAST BE AS ONE YET AGAIN.

"the fallen sorrow of the mislead lovers who seek the answers from the night that will never see the start of another beginning, searching comfort of the soul to put hearts to ease. crying out to the unknown in hope of forgotten memories to finally seize . . . so perhaps at last they may finally see that only together from the dark be free; find the world and love they were ment to see . . . and maybe die together and become one as they were ment to be."

SORROW . . . and pain is all that is here now, this vacant void that i've tried to remain hidden is finally begun to show. the demon within soon to complete its final toll against my soul. it has proven once and for all that i was not strong enough to defeat it . . . it laid dormant till it decided to take what was left of me . . .

LANORA . . . . I HAVE FAILED YOU.

i have failed others . . . including my-self . . . but i can not fight what is stronger . . . i must continue my final times with this burden stained on my heart, alone as it has, and sadly will be.

my mind can no longer take the haunted imagination other half of my sorrow . . . the pain has become to overpowering now . . . each moment the pain in my heart nearly seems to quietly calling me to the grave of my regrets.

i will one day die knowing what i could of had but refused . . . by that point it will be too late.

i will fade away once again . . . with nothing but my thoughts . . . memory will be erased for good and i will live on with those like me . . . those who had no other way out . . . . no hope . . . NO . . . . OTHER.

(this dark place i seem never to escape from, im slowly dying within)

this NIGHTMARE from the sleeping of years before . . .

i think its finally time to say good-bye to it all who have entered, to every shadow ive ever casted . . . to every single memory of the once was . . . to the corpse in the mirror, may the reflection never see again . . . my quest for neveah . . . . but most of all . . . .

you lanora . . . by now you will have no memory of what we once shared . . . what we once felt.

i want you to know that never once did i ever stop thinking of you, you haunted me until i couldn't breathe anymore . . . you were my reason . . . i loved you more than any person could . . . i gave up my world to find you . . . i believed we would find each other somehow . . . but now . . . . i have failed.

the hourglass is almost near done, and the winter where we meet is the place i must return to if i am ever to see you again; even then, i may not find you.

soon i will forever be trapped here, never to awake, never to kiss you . . . never to feel your heart with mine . . . never to walk with you across our love that was what i believed to be one of kind . . .

never to lay out in the quietness of the snow . . . you were the only one worth being cold for.

that i would embrace the demon, and the cancer all over again for one smile . . . i know i will never love anyone again . . .

you were magic that only few in this world and the next ever have . . . and i turned my back on you.

the first time i saw you, i knew that the world i once had would no longer be . . . your kiss brought me back to life, and woke me up from the dark abyss of depression from which now i have returned.

i dont have much longer, as i make my final step toward the edge . . . this was all for you . . . i hope one night you somehow find this and know i am forever eternally sorry . . .

WELL, IT IS CERTAIN NOW THAT THESE PAGES SADLY ARE ALL I HAVE TO ENDURE . . . I HAVE BEEN AND THROUGH THE TEDIOUS BOUNDS OF THE ETERNAL WAR THAT SEEMS NO LONGER WORTH THE BATTLE NOR THE FIGHT. MAYBE IT HAS ALWAYS BEEN EVIDENT THAT I WOULD RETURN TO MY STORY AND THE PAGES THAT HAVE BECOME THE ONLY PURPOSE I HAVE.

THE SLEEPLESS CAPSUEL I HAVE BEEN CONCEALED IN WILL SOON BE MY PERMANENT RESTING PLACE, THE ON-GOING NIGHTMARE THAT HAS MANIPULATED MY SOUL . . . FORCED DARKNESS INTO MY HEART HAS BECOME WHAT I HAVE ALWAYS FEARED;NOT WELCOMED. MAY IT CONSUME ME TILL THE BRINK OF MY DESTRUCTION . . . .

THE SECRET THAT I HAVE BURIED ONCE UPON A WORLD OF SNOW DEEP WITHIN A GRAVE OF SHADOWS IM AFRAID WILL NEVER TRUELY STAY BELOW;AS THE CASKET CALLS ME WITH EVERY WHISPER THAT I HAVE TRIED TO IGNORE FOR AS LONG AS MEMORY ALLOWS, THE FIGHT IS NO LONGER WORTH THE COST OF EXISTENCE.

"AS IT ALL FELL APART AND I GREW CLOSER TO THE FORSAKEN UNKNOWN . . . I COULDN'T HELP NOT TO DWELL ON THE GHOSTS THAT LEAD ME HERE TO SUBMISSION."—IV

HOW DIFFERENT THE SKY HAS BECOME NOW, HOW IN A SINGLE MOMENT YOU WAIT FOR THE HEART TO PART . . . IM READY.

I CAN'T CONTINUE WITH YOU FROM HERE ON OUT . . . I MUST BATTLE ON ALONE. WISHING ON STARS THAT NO LONGER SHINE THE WAY FOR US WILL ONLY MAKE THIS HARDER.

THE MEMORIES YOU LET ME SHARE I SHALL ALWAYS HOLD TENDER UNTIL THE SLEEP OF ME . . . SOON WE'LL BE DEPARTED BY THE COURSE UNKNOWN . . . AND THE LINGERING HAUNT OF YOU WILL RESIDE WITHIN ALWAYS TO BE FOUND WHEN NEEDED.

I MUST NOW CRY THE TEARS I FEARED I NEVER WOULD . . . AS YOU GO ON WITH YOUR LIFE WITHOUT ME . . . JUST MY HEART AND OUR MEMORIES THAT I HOPE YOU KEEP WITH YOU NO MATTER WHERE YOU GO, AND KNOW THAT YOU WILL ALWAYS BE WITH ME . . . IN WINTER OR NOT.

IF YOU EVER WANT OUR SOULS TO RE-CONNECT AND OUR HEARTS TO MERGE AS THEY ONCE HAVE . . . . AND YOU WANT NOTHING ELSE . . . I SHALL ALWAYS BE IN THAT MEMORY WHERE WE FIRST KISSED . . . I WILL BE THERE READY TO RELIVE THE LOVE AND PAIN OF OUR MAGIC CAPSUEL . . . . I'LL BE WAITING.
THIS WAS NEVER THE INTENSION OF THE FORSAKEN FEW, NEVER THE WAY I EVER THOUGHT ID FIND YOU.

HIDING FROM THE PAST ONE DREAMLESS NIGHT AT A TIME . . . . OVERCOME THE SORROW, FORGET YOUR FEAR UNLESS YOU

WANT TO DIG YOUR GRAVE FAR AWAY FROM HERE.

TELL ME IF THIS RAGE WILL EVER GO AWAY, BELIEVE THESE NIGHTS WILL SOON FADE.

THAT THIS ALTER STATE WILL WELCOME CHANGE;THIS JOURNEY
NEVER TO BE IN VEIN.

TO EVER KNOW AND TO FORGET THE MISTAKES IVE MADE . . . TO
KNOW MAYBE SOME HOW, SOME WAY I AM THE SOUL

WORTH THE SAVE;WORTH THE STRUGGLE TO EVER SEE AND
REMEMBER ANOTHER DAY.

"AS I STOOD AT THE EDGE LOOKING AT THE FOURTH COMING, MY
HEART GAVE WAY;MY MIND BLANK . . . . THE CHILLING WHISPER OF
CHANGE RAN MY SOUL MOURGE COLD . . . . THE LIGHT GREW DIM;
THE FEAR HAD RETURNED!"

-IV

WHEN THE SNOW HIT GROUND, IT BROUGHT MORE THAN JUST COLD TO THIS TOWN. I WATCHED AND WAITED BEHIND GLASS KNOWING THAT ONCE THIS MOMENT PASSED THERE WAS NO POINT OF RETURN NOR LOOKING BACK.

"SHE ENTERED MY WORLD WITHOUT QUESTION, SHE LOVED WITHOUT ANSWER;SHE SAVED ME FROM THE ENDLESS GRAVE AND RESCUED ME FROM DARKNESS WITH OUT REASON TO SHOW ME THE WAY THROUGH THE NIGHTS AND TORMENT, SO THAT I MAY SEE IN TIME THE LIGHT OF A NEW DAY."

-IV

"LOVE IS THE FABRICATED GHOST THAT HAUNTS THE MINDS OF THE LOST, LOVE HAS NO REAL NAME NOR FACE. IT IS THE MYSTIC FOG THAT ROLLS IN THEN DISAPPEARS INTO THE HEARTS OF THE WEAK"

-THE CORPSE IN THE MIRROR

"YOUR QUEST ADJACENT . . . . TASTE THE UN-STOPPING, INFRINGING THE DEAD AND TAINTING THE SOULS . . . ASSAIL THE WORLD ON THE OTHER-SIDE. SLEEP WITH NOT REHABILITATE THE MIND NO MORE AND THE SURVIVORS OF THE MAJESTIC ARE FAR AND FEW. THE TORTURED SOULS ATTEST TO HIS POWERS . . . HIDING WILL ONLY PROLONG YOUR CAPTURE. DIVULGE THE SECRET THAT WILL REVEAL YOUR SORROW."

—my SORROW

"I HAVE BETRAYED MY OWN FOR THE SAKE OF THE LOST. CURSE ME TO THE DEPTHS BELOW SO I MAY KNOW THE STRUGGLE THAT THE OTHERS KNOW . . . . I SHOULD OF TORN OUT THIS SHAPE INSIDE LONG BEFORE THIS TIME. FORGIVE ME!"

THE PRISON THEY CHOOSE FOR ME SEEMS ALL BUT TO COMFORTABLE NOW . . . .

THE OTHER-SIDE ISNT TO FAR OR NEAR, THE FREEDOM AND LOVE I SEEK WILL SADLY NEVER APPEAR.

IF NO ONE SHALL HELP OR BELIEVE THE WORDS I SPEAK, MAY HE CAPTURE AND DEVOUR THE MINDS AND SOULS OF THE NON-

BELIEVERS AND THE WEAK. MY CHANCE WAS VANISHED LONG AGO . . . EVEN WITH ESCAPE I HAVE NO WHERE LEFT TO GO AND

NOTHING BUT ETERNAL TORMENT TO SHOW.

COUNTLESS NIGHTS HERE;TRAPPED FOREVER.

THE FROZEN CLOCK THAT MAY NEVER BE FIXED . . .

I DARE NOT ASK ANY OTHER TO SHARE THE CLOCK WITH ME THAT CANT BE REPAIRED.

IN THIS TOWN WHERE THE NIGHTS SEEM TO NEVER-END AND MY WILL TO CONTINUE SLOWLY BEGINS TO BEND BECAUSE YOU

REALIZE HERE YOU TRUELY BECOME ALONE AND YOU NEVER HAVE
FAMILY OR FRIENDS. WHERE IN EVEN IN DEATH YOU SHALL

NEVER BREAK APART;NEVER WITNESS AN END OR A START. SEARCH
ALL ETERNITY FOR THE REST OF YOUR SOUL IN HOPES ONE

NIGHT YOU MAYBE ABLE TO DISCOVER AND REPAIR THE MISSING
PIECES OF THE LONG FORGOTTEN HEART. VENTURE ONWARD.

FIND THE WILL AND THE MUST NO MATTER THE COST, OTHERWISE BE
DOOMED TO BECOME ONE OF THE LOST.

I HAVE CREATED THIS BECAUSE IT WAS YOU ALL ALONG THAT FORCED ME HEART TO SHATTER. THE SHALLOW SENSE OF SELF IDENTIY THROUGH OUT THESE PAGES WAS THE ONLY WAS TO GET RID OF YOU ONCE AND FOR ALL. YOU WERE THE DEMON FOR WHICH NO EXERCISM COULD DESTORY;THE CANCER FOR WHICH THERE WAS NO CURE.

YOU BROUGHT THIS IMPENDING MISERY TO MY WORLD, YOU ARE THE RESON I WALK ACROSS THE SANDS OF SOMNAMBULISM;CRY WITH NO TEARS.

I WILL SACRIFICE NO MORE IN YOUR NAME, I WILL NO LONGER BE THE CORPSE IN THE MIRROR WITH NO FACE. THERE MUST BE ANOTHER OUT THERE FOR ME . . . SOMEONE TO HELP THROUGH ALL THIS AND IF NOT, I WILL WELCOME THE GRAVE REGRET-LESS KNOWING THAT I DID IT WITH FREEDOM.

YOU WILL NO LONGER BE THE LINGERING HAUNT OF MY NOW IS . . . OR THE ONCE WAS. WHO EVER LANORA IS, ONE THING IS CERTAIN . . . . YOU ARE NOT HER!

NOW THE ONLY THING LEFT TO DO IS DECIDE WHERE TO GO FROM HERE . . . .

VIA
~~DOLOROSA~~

for as much as our love was doomed from the start of the memory, her face will always be the haunt that follows me on my path.

always be the miss that will hurt more than the walk across the bottom i must do alone.

as far as memory has it, never was there ever a soul to counter mine, never to accept the price of evil that hid within the blood of this prison.

my demon was born from those before me, or so i thought.

perhaps it came from a transfusion of will from a early stage of time.

or maybe it was acquired from the downfall of winter,
or the loss of lanora

i cant fight what i am becoming, i cant fight the path of the forsaken nor the lost.

the will is no longer within, in time the truth will be told. i pray that the sorrow will forgive me, show me mercy for the sins of my monster.

the part of me that wants to find lanora and naveah seem to be slowly dying.

the crying soul has no more left to say. the almost deteriorated heart has no more strength.

the hourglass soon to have no more sand;the lantern no more light to guide.

why? is all that dwells between the torment and the ambivalence nightmares

the nefarious manipulator will soon come and fill the disused heart of the steadfast that roam the world above.

the invidious depression that has spawned from the Via Dolorosa has made certain my final hour, my final resting place will be uniquely

placid with the other objectionable corpses that i shall share the hollow
sepulcher.

if i had tears to give, i would ungrudgingly allocate them to all who
i have kept chained in memory; if i could locate them and release all,
i would begin with the first dream to ever become a nightmare
that saw reality.

id rather be a corpse than spend one more minute with you and the rest
of the purposeless shadows you accordance your self with.
they may be able to inveigle your soul into believing nothing lies beyond
this world, i will follow no more.

FINDING WINTER

its strange, that even after all this time . . . my heart still feels as if it has never had a single beat.;the cold still gets to me as it did the first time. once upon a memory, i remember walking down a long empty street surrounded by only trees of autumn. The colors where as beautiful as i'd have ever witnessed, the leaves blew in the wind all around me . . . the air was friendly and welcoming like change should. i could feel the warmth from the season whispering to me, asking me to embrace it . . . and i DID. The road stretched on forever but it didn't matter, i knew if i had to i could walk this path until the end . . . I would so . . . .

after countless steps, houses began to come into focus and although i wasn't quite certain of the images, it all seemed familiar like fairy tale once told at an early stage of time to calm my fear of the night outside my window.
then just when i was about to bypass, there it was . . . my house from along ago . . . the only house covered with snow amongst the rest . . . it was then i knew that . . . . THAT was were i was meant to go.

that WINTER was where my soul was meant to reside, i could never forget . . . i could never escape what was meant to be . . . that only the Snow could ever make my heart beat . . . that i no longer needed to venture down that street because i had finally found was there all along within me.

"THE UNWORTHY"

maybe i should of known all along, i trusted you with my love and life! you swore to me that you would stay and follow me until the end of darkness, i hope no mercy on you. that your nightmare be as painful as is mine . . . .

i now know i put my-self here, i don't blame the sorrow anymore or any other who came and left my-side . . . i never deserved the love of another i've never had. for as long as i can remember i have endured the suffering alone . . . all who have entered my world have abandoned me with reason. i understand that my grave was never meant for escape . . . for my casket to be nailed closed for all of eternity never to be reopened; although i understand . . . being able to accept is the painful truth i don't know if i can bare anymore.

i know now why that child built that castle within the sand . . . i understand the purpose and reason finally . . . when i decide to sleep, that will be the only darkness i will ever allow again!

the sacifice of so much for the unknowing . . . uncertain if my quest was for lanora or neveah . . . the most important ghost i seek i know now is of my-self. the doubt will always be buried within the abyss of my hollow heart.

"you were supposed to be my life! not this . . . . you promised me at the start you would always watch over me, not leave me in ruins! searching the darkest regions of my mind and hell trying to find you . . . why did you turn your wings and heart against me? that winter was our refuge . . . the playground of innocence, our second chance of walking through the eternal heaven of Re-Birth."

since birth the cancer that dwelled behind and nearly consumed my heart was the for-shadowing of depression to come . . . i have always been and always be the unworthy . . . .

first, the child not worthy of parents . . . then the teen not worthy of friendship, now after all this time . . . the man not worthy of LOVE; the trapped soul not worthy of freedom.

"IT WAS THERE, IN THAT EXCACT MOMENT . . . STANDING WITHIN THE SNOW LOOKING UP THE WHITE SKY THAT NOTHING WOULD EVER BE THE SAME AFTER THIS. IT WAS THEN I REALIZED WHAT I WANTED FROM MY EXISTENCE.

FOR I WERE TO LIVE IN ANOTHER MEMORY AND WORLD,BUT . . . DIE AND HAVE MY SOUL REST IN WINTER."

THE NIGHT WAS CALM, THE AIR WAS WELCOMING AS IT EVER WAS FOR WINTER. I WALKED FOR WHAT SEEMED LIKE MY ENTIRE CHILDHOOD, THE SOUND OF DEAD LEAVES COULD BE HEARD ALL AROUND KEEPING ME COMPANY AS I CONTINUED TOWARD MY DESTINATION UNKNOWN.

THE WIND WAS WHISPERING TO ME, TRYING TO COMFORT ME . . . . LETING ME KNOW THAT SOON . . . . IT WOULD SNOW. THERE WAS NOTHING MORE BEAUTIFUL THAN WHEN THE WORLD AROUND ME WAS COVERED IN WHITE.

MY MIND WAS PLAYING BACK MEMORIES OF THE NO LONGER IS . . . . THE DEATHS IVE COME TO WITNESS, THE LOSS OF THOSE CLOSE . . . THE TIMES THAT I WOULD NEVER SEE AGAIN . . . . HAVING NO HOME TO CALL MY OWN ANYMORE . . . NOT HAVING PARENTS TO HELP THROUGH THE PAIN THAT SURFACED FROM BELOW THE DEPTHS.

BEING ALONE BY THAT POINT DIDNT BOTHER ME AS MUCH . . . YOU GET USE TO NOT HAVING ANYONE. THE SNOW WAS ALL I NEEDED.

I COULD FEEL THAT ANY SECOND THE HEAVENS WOULD OPEN AND RELEASE THE ONLY MIRACLE I'D HAVE EVER SEEN.

THEN I REMEMBERED A SECRET SPOT . . . . ONE HIDDEN DEEP DOWN BY THE OCEAN WHERE NO ONE COULD EVER FIND ME . . . . OVER THE HILLS AND DOWN UNTIL FINALLY RESTING UPON A ROCK OVER LOOKING MILES OF DARK ENDLESS OCEAN WITH LIGHTS FROM LAND UNKNOWN IN THE DISTANCE . . . . JUST THE TRANQUIL SOUND OF WAVES SOFTLY KISSING THE ROCKS BELOW ME . . . AND THE FLAWLESS MOON ABOVE IN THE STARLESS SKY CASTING ITS REFLECTION UPON THE WATER TO SAY HI.

YES, I WOULD WAIT THERE FOR THE SNOW TO COME DOWN . . . . AND WHEN IT STARTED TO SNOW THE WORLD AROUND ME WAS SO BEAUTIFUL I COULD NOT FULLY DESCRIBE IN DETAIL.

I WOULD SIT THERE OUT AMONGST THE OCEAN AND THE QUITNESS OF THE SNOW UNTIL MY FINAL BREATH.

THE PLACE WHERE MY MEMORIES BEGAN WOULD BE THE PLACE MY MEMORIES ENDED.

Edwards Brothers, Inc.
Thorofare, NJ USA
May 26, 2011